The month of January flew by in a flurry of activities. The former chief of police now police consultant of the sheriff's department was still reeling from the events of January.

As a veteran lawman, Jack was fully aware of the fact that during the Holidays the crime rate went up. However, the January crime wave in Belleville took everyone by surprise.

First, there was the robbery that the Sheriff and Jack handled with flair, then there was an accidental death that turned out to be a revenge murder in disguise, then there were the break-ins during Christmas eve mass.

At least a dozen homes were broken into while most of the Belleville population were in church celebrating midnight mass.

In reality, by a large metropolis standard, their crime wave wouldn't make anyone in the big city bat an eye. But to the small town of Belleville, population under three thousand, it was quite unnerving for them to have to deal with so many crimes all at once.

Things seemed to have calmed down now, it was February and Jack Bourgeois was enjoying his morning breakfast with his friend and Housekeeper Miss Anita.

The morning delight was plantain boiled and a red herring omelet. Miss Anita's meals were simple, but to Jack's taste they were as tasty as a meal prepared by a cordon blue chef, and he should know since he'd travel extensively, for his work and for pleasure.

The coffee never stop, in fact, Jack was on his third cup. The strong brew was just as he preferred it, strong and sweet. He was reading today's paper as Miss Anita cleared the table.

The two had formed a bond, a family of sorts over the year Jack left in Belleville. Sent there to solve a case by the elected president himself, Jack Bourgeois found himself so enthralled with Belleville's small-town charm that he ended up moving there.

He was hired as a consultant for the sheriff's department and was independently wealthy since he owned a security firm along with his best friend Rene Cadet. He was a silent partner, while Rene ran the day to day of their business.

Things were doing well with the business, they'd signed on more accounts, and the new branch office Jack opened in Au Cap was starting to show a profit. Jack's private life was also doing well. He'd been dating Olga, a policewoman from one town over, and their relationship was just what the doctor ordered.

Jack drove to the sheriff's station soon after. The last few days, things had reverted back to peaceful and quiet. The sheriff had not called him in so Jack assumed that the status quo remained.

When he entered the office the sheriff was waiting for him. "Bonjour Jack, I was waiting for you." "Bonjour sheriff, what do you need me to do? Just come with me.

Outside in the parking lot, the sheriff informed Jack that they were called to the scene of a crime at a dress shop. It was only a couple of blocks away near the plaza.

The store displayed valentines day decorations. The front mannequin was dressed in lingerie. Conservative, in comparison to the kind Jack had seen during the course of his career.

The owner Ginette Milien was a smiling middle-aged woman, gently rounded with a pretty face, and a dazzling smile. She had a gap in between her front teeth, something Jack quite cute.

The woman had a maternal vibe about him that reminded Jack of his own mother. The robber came in last night and stole three hundred dollars worth of clothes.

For the next hour, Jack and the sheriff gathered information about Ginette, her two employees, and their families.

"I started the shop after my husband's death five years ago." "My children are grown and live in Au Cap with their families." "I have a couple of boys, and they are both married, five grandchildren if you can believe it."

She had a smile from ear to ear. Jack felt his heart squeeze. His own mother had barely gotten to see Jacky, Jack's daughter from his failed marriage.

His daughter was the best thing that he'd ever done, Jack thought. No amount of success can ever compare to the satisfaction he felt when he'd become a father.

Jack and the sheriff pored over the information they had gathered. They spent a couple of hours walking around the store and gathering information. It wasn't going to be so easy, since the items were probably sold, or pawned at this time.

Jack got used to Belleville's way of life. The cases he handled were mostly misdemeanors, and petty crimes but every now and then, things heated up.

Jack made a plan with his girlfriend Olga who worked as a beat cop in au Cap but was considering accepting a position as sheriff deputy of Milo. Jack encouraged her to accept the position, she was really good at her job and wasn't getting the recognition she deserved as yet.

Jack was taking things slowly with Olga. They'd both had bad relationships and understood each other. Jack's marriage wasn't bad per se, the woman he'd married loved him very much, unfortunately, his wife's love hadn't been enough to help him forget his true love, Karine the one woman who'd made him feel things he'd never felt before.

He'd had a few casual relationships with women since his divorce, and he'd ensured that every woman he'd dated knew that he wasn't looking for a wife. Of course, a few believed they could change his mind. He didn't like having awkward breakups, but once a woman expected more than he could give, there was no other choice.

He liked Olga very much, and they were attracted to each other. She was pretty, she was smart, and she understood him.

She was well aware that they were keeping each other's company to ease their loneliness. Her being in law enforcement also meant that she understood his work and what it meant to him.

The last few months were good for them both of them. It was about to be valentine's day and if they had the time they would grab dinner and spend some private time together. But there was no pressure.

That evening Jack had dinner with Miss Anita his housekeeper and friend. They talked about their respective day and ate the day's delight as Jack referred to the older woman's food.

Miss Anita was a gifted cook worthy of a cordon blue. Jack had eaten in diverse eateries in the world yet Miss Anita's food was one of the best he'd ever had.

Their relationship felt like more a mother and child connection instead of what they really were, employer-employee. Miss Anita was one of Jack's closest friends despite the fact that he was also friends with some of the most prominent citizens of Belleville.

Miss Anita told Jack about her cousin coming soon for a visit. Jack was thrilled for her. Miss Anita lived alone and Jack was glad that she'd have some company. Miss Anita never married. She was once engaged, but the breakup caused her so much pain, that she swore off men after that.

Jack knew all about heartbreak. Watching the love of his life marry a man she didn't love broke Jack's heart irremediably. Still, he loved Karin, he thought about her all the time and wondered what their lives would have been like if he had chosen him instead of Raymond.

It didn't matter anymore he told himself. Around Valentine's day, he often felt this way, although it would do him any good since Karine built her life with another man, and Jack tried to do the same.

His marriage failed, it was mostly his fault, but he wasn't sorry he'd gotten married, out of that union his daughter Jacky, his most precious treasure was born.

He wasn't the father he'd wanted to be, but he loved his daughter and would do anything for her. She lived far away, but she had his heart, and his devotion just the same.

The next day, Jack and the Sherrif were called to another store. The thieves stole a bunch of lingerie amount to five hundred dollars.

The owners of the sore a married couple, Myrna and Louis Adam were having a hard time comprehending what happened.

Louis was perplexed. "I don't understand sheriff Dumas my wife and I moved to Belleville because we were told it was a sleepy little town were nothing exciting happened and the crime rate was so low that it was almost non existent."

Jack in the mean time looked around the store as the techs lifted finger prints and id other things pertaining to their jobs. Monsieur Adam would soon realized that there were crimes everywhere, as long as they were human beings living in a area, there would be some type of crime committed.

The next few days were spent investigating every one in the Adams' life, including the few clients they had. They were new to town, and their business was young. Jack and the sheriff were doing their due diligence when a third clothing store was robbed.

That was when they decided to put surveillance on the remaining clothing stores that hadn't been robbed. If the robbers continued their pattern one of the stores were going to be robbed.

Jack wasn't surprised when the Sherrif requested him as backup at the store location were he'd parked his car down the street to avoid being seen by the robbers. Since the store was situated in a residential neighborhood, the sheriff parked his car near a house down the street to the store.

He allowed the two people to get inside first before he called for back up, got out of his car to catch them pushing merchandise into large garbage bags.

The sheriff arrested the pair who turned out to be a man a woman in their twenties. Jack got there just in time to hear the sheriff read them their rights, and put them in the back of a squad car.

"Well, sheriff, I guess our work is done here." "Not so fast, I'm afraid we still have the owners to visit and informed them of their lucky break." It was a rare occurrence but it was quite a thrill to be able to stop a crime in it's course. It was a lawman's dream come true.

One

Jack Bourgeois woke up brusquely from the nightmare. He sat upright in the middle of the king-size b bed. The nightmare that plagued him ever since he'd gotten shot a few months back was robbing him from sleep again.

Eleven months earlier, Jack was the chief of police of Delmas, a middle class section of Port Au Prince. Under his direction, the community of Delmas had seen a significant reduction in crimes.

A career police man, Jack had joined the police corps right after he'd completed his high school studies. He'd thrived at the academy attracting the attention of diverse police chiefs and captains who wanted him to work at their precinct.

Jack was a bit disoriented, it took him a minute to realize that he wasn't home. No, he was in Belleville, the small town in the Northern part of the country. And he remembered too, his reasons for being here.

The moon was shining into his room as his eyes adjusted it to the semi darkness. He turned on the bedside lamp, then he got out of bed. Jack inserted his feet into thong sandals in front of the bed and walked his way toward to kitchen, turning on the light before he made his way to the refrigerator.

At six feet two inches, Jack was an impressive sight. His dark skin glowed with health. He ate well, and exercised. His enjoyed running and swimming. Now he dragged his feet. His squared face was tight with sleep, but he knew that he wasn't going to fall asleep again. Once he was up, that was it.

After pouring himself a glass of cold water, Jack walked to the kitchen table and sat down. He'd been in Belleville only a week, and despite the welcome wagon, Jack couldn't wait to get back to Port Au Prince.

He wanted his life back. He simply needed to go back to his routine. Since his divorce from Ginette, his work has been his life. The divorce was his fault, he shouldn't have married Ginette, knowing that he didn't love her, at least not the way a man loved the woman he was suppose to spend the rest of his life with. He'd only felt that kind of love once, and the woman in question was now married to another man. A vile criminal at that.

Jack got up abruptly, he didn't want to think about this again. Karin's marriage to Raymond Duquette had tormented Jack for years. Even during his own marriage. He and Karin were childhood friends who grew up in the same neighborhood. They had one think in common. They were being raised by single mothers.

But while Jack had been an only child, Karin had three sisters. Jack never knew his father. Karin's mother was married to an army lieutenant who divorced her after fifteen years of marriage to marry a younger woman.

Soledad, Karin's mother became bitter, she had a great life as a lieutenant's wife, and was reduced to having to work to take care of her four daughters. Jack mother on the other hand never had the help of the man who'd gotten her pregnant at twenty. She'd moved to Port Au Prince when Jack was five years old. She worked as a maid to keep a roof over their heads and food on the table.

Karin's mother baked wedding cakes to make ends meet, and made a decent living at it. Jack and Karin became friends when his mother worked for Soledad one summer. The arrangement didn't work, Soledad wasn't punctual with payments while being very exigent with her expectations of Marie Lourdes.

Marie Lourdes was force to seek employment elsewhere earning Soledad as an enemy because of it, but Jack remained friends with the girls, especially Karin. For the life of him he didn't understand why all these memories were coming back to him.

It's true that the fresh air was doing him good. The small picturesque town was truly enchanting. It was five in the morning, and the only noise Jack could hear was the chirping of the cicadas.

Since he was up anyway, Jack decided to do some work. He walked to the percolator and prepared some coffee. His best friend and business partner Rene Cadet was the CEO of their national security company. It wasn't well known that Jack was independently wealthy. He worked as a police officer because it was his passion, not because of the meager paycheck.

Once the coffee was ready, Jack poured a generous of sugar into it. He took it with him to the living room where the file laid open on the coffee table. Miss Anita his housekeeper would be in soon enough. The older woman was very punctual.

She was also a very good housekeeper. Roland Dumas Belleville's sheriff had hired her to take care of the house that he'd rented for Jack. Jack hoped that his stay in Belleville will be a short.

As it is, he didn't even understand why he'd allowed Lucien Martin to rope him into this Jack thought now. But the truth is, Jack was desperate to to get his job back. While he was convalescing, the newly elected Lucien Martin had the brilliant idea of replacing Jack with his illegitimate son Rigaud Martin.

To think that he'd voted for the man. Jack regretted that now. Lucien Martin a former college professor who taught social science at the Universite d etats. For years he was a militant, a peaceful fighter for the right of the people. He'd been arrested countless times for standing up to the diverse dictators who'd become president the last three decades.

Jack who'd always been a skeptic worked during Lucien Martin's rallies many times helping to keep things civil. But there was something about he man that pulled Jack in. So when Lucien Martin threw his hat into the political ring, Jack supported his efforts with anonymous donations, and on the day of the election, Jack proudly voted for him.

But like most politician, he was a disappointment. It wasn't just rumors of his affairs that bothered Jack. It was the blatant disregard for the law. He'd assigned a high level position to his love child to calm down his former student, who happen to be Rigaud Martin's mother.

It wasn't office gossip either. While Jack was recuperating from the bullet wound he'd suffered to save Lucien Martin's life. The newly elected president replaced Jack by his rookie son who was barely out of the academy. It was frankly an insult. If he'd replaced Jack with one of his own man, a career police man who knew how to do the job, Jack would have let it go.

The young man was an incompetent idiot was putting every once in danger with each passing day. He put Jack' men at risk, as well as the public they were suppose to be protecting

And that's not to mention the fact that Rigaud Martin was going to destroy Jack lifework. It took him years to get his precinct to become one of the more efficient ones in the country.

Once Jack was better, he'd made an appointment to see the president. However, it became clear that the politician was avoiding him when on three occasions Jack drove all the way to the palace only to be told the president wasn't there, or he was in an urgent meeting.

So Jack decided to beat the man at his own game. He bribed a couple of guards who were more than happy to divulge Lucien Martin's business. One evening Jack scaled the back wall of the palace while the guards were busy taking a cigarette break.

Jack silently made his way to Lucien Martin's office, and he didn't hear Jack coming since the man was busy with a young secretary when Jack entered his office. The two broke apart, the young woman no more than twenty two had the decency to look embarrassed. She rushed out with her head low.

Lucien Martin however looked annoyed and proud. He seemed bothered, yet there was this int of a smile on his thin face. "Captain Bourgeois, though I appreciate your saving my life, I still think you should follow protocol and make an appointment in other to see me."

Was this following protocol, Jack thought of the scene he'd just walked in a minute ago. But he kept the thought to himself. It was disappointing to confirm Lucien Martin's philandering ways, but he had more pressing business.

"Mr. President I made three appointments to see you, and each time it seems you were extremely busy." "So, I was force to come up with other alternatives." "I'm here about my job." "You told me yourself that your son was there as interim chief, until I recuperated." "I' am healthy, and fit and you can call my doctors if you want, they will tell you that they gave me a clean bill of health."

"I don't need to Captain, you wouldn't lie about something like this." "However, I cannot give you your job at this present time." "Why not," Jack asked his tone more aggressive than he intended it to be."

He had a dangerous look on his face that made the politician cringe. "Because I promised my son that he could keep the job for a year, after that I'll find someplace else to post him."

"So you lied to me then." "Not exactly." "What does that mean sir, you either lie to me, or you didn't." Jack was getting angry, and things were getting out of hand Lucien Martin thought. While Jack had the reputation of being a fair and law abiding police man. Lucien Martin had heard stories. He wasn't one to cross. I'm already making enough enemies. Jack is wealthy and well connected, he might cause me trouble.

"Since you seem desperate to regain your post Captain, I have a big problem on my hand that only a seasoned investigator such as yourself can help me with." "What is it this time sir." Ignoring Jack tone of voice, Lucien Martin went on. "I've you heard of the case of the disappearing women of Belleville."

Who hasn't heard of that Jack thought. He stood there his fist tight, while Lucien Martin remained seated. But he relaxed once he heard of the case that everyone was talking about. "Yes, I've read about it in the paper." "Okay, then I'll make you a deal." "If you can resolve the case of the missing women, I'll pull my son out your chair myself."

"Take a seat captain, you don't have to stand guard." Jack sat down. "Okay sir, for me to agree to do this, I need your word in writing, and I need a couple of witnesses." Lucien Martin look wounded. "These are my terms, if you want my help with the Belleville situation." "You don't trust my word Captain, Lucien Martin." He looked straight into Jack' eyes, daring the lawman to to state his lack of trust of him clearly.

"I need things on paper, sir, this way there will not be any misunderstand, and the witnesses will be there to ensure everything is official." Jack stared him straight into the eyes, his dark brown eyes not blinking. He wasn't about to fall for the same trick, if he were to get his job back, he'd have to corner Lucien Martin into keeping his word.

" Okay then I'll have the papers ready tomorrow, and I'll provide the witnesses." "No sir, I will provide the witnesses." "I'll see you tomorrow around ten O'clock." "When did I loose your trust Jack?" Lucien Martin asked as he walked Jack to the door." "Do I really need to answer that sir?"

The next morning, Jack and his best friend Rene Cadet, as well as judge George Mars witness the president sign the contract stating he'd reinstate Jack to his former position of Captain of the precinct of Delmas as soon as he resolved the Belleville missing woman case.

That afternoon, Jack called Sheriff Roland Dumas to introduce himself, and let him know that he was on his way. The next morning Jack made all the arrangement to travel that afternoon.

He drove five hours and made it to Belleville at dusk. He followed the directions given to him by Roland Dumas and met him at the Belleville Sheriff's office. The fifty year old Roland Dumas was short and stocky, he seemed to have kind eyes, although Jack knew he had to be some kind of tough to have reach this degree of success in his career.

The two shook hands, after introducing themselves. Although Jack didn't need introduction since his face was plastered over every Haitian newspapers, even on some international periodical carried the news, the day he took an assassin's bullet meant for the newly elected Haitian president.

The sheriff asked Jack to follow him, he took Jack to the house he'd rented for Jack with the money Jack had deposited on his account. The house was just three blocks away from the station. Jack was already thinking that he might walk to work some times.

The sun was setting and he couldn't see the town in all of its splendor, although he'd never travel north of Haiti, Jack knew Belleville to be among on of the most beautiful small towns in the country. It was also one of these towns with a very low crime rate, which is why the disappearance of five young woman had alarmed everyone.

The Sheriff unlocked the door, and turn on the lights, then led Jack in. "This is what I could find on such short notice." Jack looked around, it's a pretty good he said, once he'd looked around. The house had indoor plumbing and indoor kitchen. "Miss Anita the housekeeper I hired for you will be here in the morning." She's an older woman, a spinster who spend her life helping married woman feed their husbands, and raise their children."

"She sounds like a good person." "She is, don't let her brusque manner fool you." "Wait till you taste her cooking." "The woman really have her ten fingers, it's really too bad that she never married." Jack mind was miles away, but he listened with half a ear anyway. "Rumor has it that she got her heart broken when she was young, the experience soured her on man." That seems to be going around Jack thought, remembering his own heartbreak. Once he'd seen the house, Jack decided to get started on the case that brought him to Belleville. "So, what can you tell me about the missing girls?"

"I prepared a case file, I'll get the papers from the truck," the sheriff said. Jack made his way to the refrigerator, it was well stocked. "Miss Anita got you a few things to tie you down until the morning." "I see, I think I love her already, she does her job well," "Yeah, she's efficient, and wait till you taste her food."

Jack poured a couple of glasses of lemonade from the pitcher of sweat lemonade Miss Anita had prepared for him. After gulping down the juice the sheriff left. "I'll see you in the morning." "Jack took a shower, and after wolfing down two of the sandwiches and two more glasses of lemonade, he settled down in bed with the files in hand.

By habit, he had turned the TV on since he always watched the news every night. He was pleasantly surprised to see the house was equipped with radio and television. Although he'd brought his laptop with him, Jack enjoyed watching the news on Television, or listening to it on the radio. He lived in the modern world, but some things Jack preferred them to remain the same.

After reading the basic information about the young woman, Jack made up his mind that he was going to re-interview everyone. With the sheriff's permission of course. He wouldn't want the man to think that he believed him to be incompetent. If he lasted this long as a lawman he must be good at his job.

But he needed the information first hand. There may be things that he'll see since he's coming in with fresh eyes. But there was more to this case Jack knew. He had the nagging feeling that Lucien Martin omitted something important about this. And Jack feared what it could be. The man allowed him to twist his arms, this isn't likely in any president, not even in this supposed man of the people.

After a week in Belleville, Jack realized that he'd been to one to be tricked. It wasn't that he didn't know it on the onset, but finding out that another investigator was sent before him, and had run scared back to Port Au Prince was information that he needed to have.

Lucien Martin of course wouldn't answer his calls on the day that Jack found out that Tamien Lenoire a retired police chief was sent to Belleville and nearly died of unknown causes while in Belleville. Some said he was poisoned. One things is for sure, as soon as he was well enough, Damien returned to Port Au Prince.

One Sheriff Dumas had informed him of the event, Jack tried to get in contact with former chief Lenoire. But he too wouldn't answer his phone. It was obvious that the man was avoiding Jack. Jack might have to travel and see him in person. Jack thought that the case would be resolved easily, but now, he knew better.

If a seasoned officer who was trained in the most modern ways of policing couldn't hatch it, it was going to be an uphill battle Jack knew. Whoever had poisoned him didn't want the case resolved. Jack needed to talk to Lenoire, because the attack on him meant that he was getting close.

But it was only a week and Jack wanted to see what he could do here before he intruded into the former chief's life. Now as he read the information he'd gathered himself, he couldn't help wonder if this case can ever be resolved, because he was realistic enough to know that some cases couldn't be solved.

Jack got in through the back door. The smell of fresh coffee greeted him. Miss Anita was punctual to a fault. She made it to Jack' house at six o'clock every morning. She was cordial to Jack, but kept her distance. Jack was still trying to convince her to sit down and have breakfast with him.

"Non, I can't do that, you are my employer chief Bourgeois." "You are right, Miss Anita, but there isn't any rules that say that we can't also be friends." Miss Anita looked shocked, and for a second, she couldn't speak. She simply tightened the sweater around her polyester dress.

But Jack could see that she was pleased. This classicism garbage grazed Jack temper. He might be wealthy now, but his mother too worked as a domestic to provide for him. As far as he was concerned people in the service fields were the hardest working people he knew and deserved to be respected just as much as anyone else.

Eventually Miss Anita will join him at the table to share mills. So far she's been very useful to him. Reserved at first, Jack was forced to use his charm and interrogation skills to get Miss Anita talking.

The information she'd provided him about the missing women was valuable. The family members omitted information to put their relatives in the best lights possible. But Miss Anita didn't mince words.

Through her, Jack found out that at three of the missing young woman had been fighting with her fiance right before they were missing. That was another connection that non one had made before, at least as far as Jack knew. Until he had a chance to speak to chief Lenoire, he couldn't be sure. "Bonjour Miss Anita." "Bonjour, chief Bourgeois." Jack went straight to the bathroom and took a shower.

The only thing wrong with this house is the cold water. There wasn't a water heater, and Jack was force to shower with the cold water. He showered in a hurry and rushed out. He dried himself and dress. He couldn't wait to taste whatever culinary delight Miss Anita had prepared for him. His phone rang as he was getting dressed. It was Rene Cadet his best friend and business partner. Jack figured Rene was checking up on him.

However, as soon as Jack picked up the phone, he knew that something was dreadfully wrong. He knew that his ex wife and daughter were fine since he'd spoken to both of them the day before yesterday.

His ex moved to Miami and was now happily remarried. Frank was decent man, Jack traveled specifically to Miami to meet the man right before he married his ex wife, for Jacky's sake. He adored his daughter, and if he couldn't provide the family she deserved, Jack wanted to ensure that at least she'd have a decent step father.

His daughter was growing fast. Nearly eighteen years old, Jacky was as intelligent as she was beautiful. Jack and Frank had establish a relationship of sort, and although Jack had been skeptical at first, that his ex wife new husband wanted to be friends with him, over the years, Jack realized that Frank was one of the most transparent human beings he'd ever met. He just wanted to keep the peace between them for Jacky's sake.

His daughter was all the family he had in the world. Although it was a mistake to marry a woman he didn't love, and to have married so young. Jacky made it all worthwhile. So when he heard Rene's tone of voice, his daughter was the first person who came to mind.

"Allo, Jack," Rene said his tone grave. "What's going on Rene." They've known each other for years. The two met at the academy, and became fast friend. They'd seen each other through many things during their twenty year friendship. They were each others best man, although Rene marriage was still intact, and Jack was god father to his first child.

Rene had helped him through the divorce, and living far away from his daughter. He knew about Karine, and all the sufferings that Jack has been through. In fact, Rene knew more about Karine and her delinquent husband Raymond since he'd worked the precinct nearest to their home of Petionville.

Jack had suspected that there was more to Karine's marriage to Raymond that he wasn't aware off. "I'm going to get straight to the point, Karine is in trouble." Jack sat down on the bed. He held the phone tight, a dark feeling settled over him. Outside he could hear passerby, and inside the house he heard the clatter of plates and cutlery. Miss Anita was setting the table.

The feeling of doom intensified, his chest tightened. If Rene was calling him about Karine it meant the situation was dire. His friend had done his best over the years to avoid the subject of Jack' ex girlfriend since Jack was still so hurt over Karine's rejection more than twenty years ago.

"What kind of problems?" "Raymond has been holding her hostage for more than a week." "The special drug unit has his house surrounded and he threatens to kill her if they go in." "How did I not hear of all of this?" "They were trying to keep it on the down low." "But a maid who managed to escape told the authorities that Raymond is high on drugs, and he he's been beating her for days."

Jack listened to the details of what Karine had gone through at the hands of her sadistic husband, and he knew that he had to rescue her from the man's clutches.

"I'm on my way, he said to Rene." "I need to make some calls but expect me around noon." "Are you sure, because we can turn this over to the concerned authorities Rene replied." "The concerned authorities have not rescued her in a week, I don't think they will." "Besides, won't him to feel cornered and do something desperate."

Rene understood too well what Jack meant. Men like Raymond weren't the type to allow themselves to be arrested. He'd rather die, and take his wife with him. Jack hanged up the phone and made his way to his closet. His grabbed the case containing his gun. He put a change of clothes in a small bag along with the case. Then he made a call to Au Cap. He ordered a chattered plane with destination to Port Au Prince. The plane would be ready for departure in two hours and a half, they told him after taking down his credit card information.

Miss Anita was waiting for him, the food already served. The morning delight was cornmeal with red herring and spinach and home made orange juice just the way he liked it, with ice cubes swimming in it, sugar and vanilla essence. "You don't look well," Miss Anita said. "I just heard some bad news," Jack replied. "It's nothing I can't resolve but it will take some doing."

"Do you want to tell me about it," Miss Anita said. "I will if you sit down and have breakfast with me, Miss Anita." She looked like she was about to protest. But the hopeful look on Jack' face convinced her otherwise.

Jack ended up telling her the whole story from beginning to end. Miss Anita was touched. "Go with God captain, this woman truly needs help." "I hope that you and your people capture him before he hurts her more." "I hope so too," Jack said. Miss Anita made the sign of the cross. A fervent Catholic she attended mass daily. "You'll see that God willing everything will go well.

Jack hoped so as well, since the task that laid ahead of him, was going to be challenging and dangerous.. He sent a silent prayer that things will go according to plans, and without anyone else getting hurt. But the reality was Raymond wasn't going to give up easily. And he wasn't going to just surrender and allow Karine to leave him. She was his most prize possession after all.

The trip to Au Cap went without event. It was early morning and traffic wasn't too bad. As Jack drove by the farmlands that made up the lower parts of Belleville, he couldn't help realize just how contrasting the two parts of Belleville were. Upper burgh where he now lived housed the most prominent citizens of Belleville.

Lower burgh housed the hard working farmers who produced the food and raised the cattle that made Belleville a well to do small town. The beauty of the prairie land was quite a sight. He drove to the outskirts of town and past two other small towns before he reached Au Cap.

Traffic was another matter once Jack reached the large metropolis. It was frankly a nightmare to make it to the airport. Fortunately he'd left with enough time to spare and made it to the airport with thirty minutes to spare. The young pilot was waiting to fly him to Port Au Prince. Jack introduced himself to Guy Montes and after getting over the preliminary salutations got on the plane as Guy got into the cockpit.

They made good time. Jack was in Port Au Prince an hour and forty five minutes later. The flight was a bit turbulent, but he was used to that. In the course of business, Jack took many trips all over the country and overseas. As soon as they landed Jack phone Rene. His friend was at the Airport waiting for him. Some of their best employees were with Rene.

Five of the best former police officers to be exact. Rene had offered to house his fried, but Jack declined. He didn't want to put Rene's family at risk. It was one thing for Rene to volunteer to help, and other thing for his family to get involved in something that was so dangerous.

Jack coordinated his efforts with that of the swat team that was already in place. Although they weren't pleased about his interference initially, they were forced to admit that his help was invaluable in the end.

While their job was to capture Raymond, his goal was to ensure Karine's safety. They breach in late that afternoon and since they already held the plans of the compound they were able to focus their efforts on the main house. Most of Raymond's guards had deserted them, like rats abandoning a sinking ship.

The group of twenty officers were well trained, the best of the best and they were well protected. A total of six men were arrested. Jack entered the house and followed the instructions of the maid who escaped.

He found Karin in a back room just like the maid had indicated. She lay on the floor, and when Jack noticed she wasn't moving he feared the worst. By then Raymond who was high on drugs had been subdued. His body guard after seeing two of their fellow guards shot down had surrendered.

The harden criminal hurled insults at Jack who completely ignored him. Jack frantically searched for the room until he found Karin. "Karin, he said shaking her shoulder once he made his way to her face. Once he'd actually seen her face, Jack held his breath as he checked for a pulse. It was thready but she had a pulse.

Her face was bruised and battered, one eyes seemed to be glued shut, probably from a punch. She had blood crusted at the corners of her mouth. Jack picked her up and carried her outside. Things were calming down. Raymond was sitting behind a police car with a his hands held behind his back.

"Is she dead?" The criminal asked a smile on his face. Jack ignored him once more. He wasn't about to fall into his provocation, although he'd never wanted to hurt someone more in his life. But he continued on to one of the waiting ambulances and demanded they take Karine before one of the injured guards.

Once he'd been assured that Karine was secured in, he made his way to his car parked down the hills. "Take her to Canape Vert," Jack ordered before he left for his car. "Okay chief," the Emergency Technician told him. He followed the ambulance at the same speed, and parked behind in as they brought Karin out. He was told to park elsewhere, but he made sure Karine got inside the hospital before he did so.

"How is she?" Jack asked the emergency room physician. She has fractured ribs, and from what I can see, she lost a back tooth. I'm taking her to have some ex rays done to find out more. "What more," Jack asked frustrated. "She could have internal bleeding, so we need to do more test the doctor said in a somber tone.

Jack didn't want to leave Karine alone, he still feared the worst. She was asleep by the time they allowed him to see her in the private that he'd insisted on. They'd given her some sedative for the pain. She seem to be having nightmares. She was crying in her sleep. Jack tried to soother her. "Sheww, you're safe now, Raymond can't hurt you anymore, go back to sleep." She fell asleep again. Jack called Rene who informed him that Raymond was in jail awaiting trial.

He was denied bail since he was a flight risk. Good, he thought. "How's Karine?" Rene wanted to know. "I'd like to say better, but I'm not sure." "Raymond is a savage beast, wait till I get my hands on him." "Well he is in jail now Jack, he can't hurt anyone one else."

"I hope so," Jack said then sighed. They both knew how corrupt the judicial system was in Haiti. They did their job and arrested criminals only to see them walk because of corrupt judges who put a price on their decrees. It was sickening really, but what could they do.

With each elected official there was some kind of corruption to deal with. Jack focused on the task at hand. Political climates aside, they had to ensure that Raymond couldn't get out. Because for sure next time he'd kill Karine, not to mention his many other victims.

He had a trail of blood 100 mile running behind him, and if Jack had to pull in in every favor he was owed, this time Raymond wasn't going to escape his fate. Jack wasn't going to take any chances, he called one of his best man to come and guard Karine.

Call him paranoid, but he took Raymond's last words as a threat. Since he was currently behind bars Raymond couldn't touch Karine, but Jack knew that he could hire any one of his faithful dogs to come and finish what he'd started.

Then Jack went to his office to pick up some papers. His plan was to take Karin back with him to Belleville where he could keep watch over her. She was still asleep and Jack doubted that she'd go without a fight, she was very attached to her family from what Jack remembered, and unfortunately her mother Soledad had a fierce hold on her. The woman relished ruining his daughter's lives, starting with Karine.

Her matchmaking and greed nearly cost her life, God only knew just what kind of psychological trauma all these years of abuse was going to cause Karine. Some women shouldn't be mothers because frankly women like Karine's mother Soledad weren't born with maternal instincts.

Instead of protecting Karine from harm, she send him in harm's way. To escalate social status. For money, she sold her eldest child, and at least two of the others to the highest bidders. The sisters were quite beautiful, and to Soledad it was a commodity to exploit. Here was the result.

She called the hospital to inquire about Karine, Jack told Soledad that Karine was alive, no thanks to her. She burst into tears. But Jack wasn't buying it. Those crocodile tears wouldn't convince him. Not after he learned that Soledad knew the hellish life was living with Raymond. If he was slapping her around before they were married, what was to stop him now that she was sold to him.

Karine seemed to not have a will of her own when it came to her mother. The woman uses guilt as anyone else would use water. It was as if she couldn't live without it. As if she was the only single mother in existence. What a single mother wanted most was for their children to grow up to be happy, and form the family they weren't able to provide them with.

Jack went home to pack. His home in Tabar was one of the most beautiful in the area and that was saying a lot. But ironically he spent more time traveling than in his beautiful home. He didn't care to analyze the reasons why, inside these walls that represented his success all he felt was loneliness.

Maggie his housekeeping woman and husband Gil lived on the property. Jack knew they were trustworthy they'd earn his trust long ago. So he didn't mind mind paying them the absurdly high salary since they had to support their son Gil Junior through medical school.

Three

The trip back to Belleville was short thankfully, because Karine looked as if she was about to faint for a while there. This was something new that Jack was learning about her. She's afraid to fly in an airplane. But then again, there was a lot more they didn't know about each other.

Karine was hurt, broken emotionally and physically and his goal was to nurse her back to health. After that she'd decide what she wanted to do with the rest of her life. His car was waiting for them at the airport parking spot he'd paid for.

Jack drove them to Belleville, and they made good time, only thirty five minutes despite the heavy midday traffic. Miss Anita was waiting for them. Karine kept her eyes closed during the trip, although they both knew she wasn't asleep. She didn't want to talk, and Jack didn't want to push her.

The house was permeated with the smell of food. Jack mouth watered. Miss Anita we're here, Jack shouted from the living room after locking the door behind them. Karine only had a small suitcase containing the most essentials. Jack could always take her shopping in Au Cap once she felt better, he'd told her.

"You are in for a treat," he told Karine. Miss Anita is one of the best cooks I've ever met. As if on cue Miss Anita rushed to meet them, a ready smile on her face. "Chief Bourgeois, you're back." "Yes Miss Anita, but remember before I left we agreed that you will call me Jack." Miss Anita looked away. She looked a bit flustered.

Karin had sat down. She must be exhausted he thought. "This is our guess Karine, she's gong to be with us for a while." Karine made the effort to get up, she groaned in pain. Jack helped her up, and to all of their surprise she went and kissed Miss Anita on the cheek. "Bonsoir, my name is Karine, I am a friend of Jack's." Miss Anita's face glowed, she was pleased that Karine showed her such respect. "Eh bien Miss Karine, I will do my best to make your stay agreeable."

"Thank you Miss Anita, I appreciate that, but call me Karine, I insist." With that Karin turned to Jack, I am tired, can I please go to my room." "Sure," Jack answered. "Miss Anita has your room ready." Jack looked at Miss Anita who nodded. Jack got ahead and Karin followed him down a hall way, and into a spacious room with a queen size bed at its center.

Jack had ordered the bedroom set right before he left and he was pleased to see that the furniture was delivered on time. Miss Anita who had followed them, offered to help Karine into bed. Jack left the room, to give them some space. Knowing Karine she'd be more at ease with the older woman. Miss Anita had a maternal way about her and right now Karine needed all the care she could get.

Jack busied himself in the mean time, because he was going to ensure that Karine got something in her stomach before she took the pills the doctor prescribed for the pain and the calcium to help strengthen her bone. Every time Jack saw her suffer, he felt the strong urge to hit something, or someone, who was he kidding,

Jack told himself, what he wanted to do was to heap a good beating on Raymond to make him pay for what he'd done to Karine. But he had to contained himself, he couldn't get into any kind of legal trouble right now, Karine needed his help, she needed his protection.

Jack could only hope that Raymond got what he deserved, although in the back of his mind, Jack knew that chances were Raymond might get away with this too, like he'd gotten away with many other crimes. But right now, he felt a glimmer of peace because Karine was here with him where he can keep an eye on her.

Miss Anita came back out but only to bring Karin a bowl of bouillon. Jack had the same idea, but he didn't make Karine uncomfortable. He followed behind, but didn't go in. He picked as Miss Anita spoon fed Karin who had difficulty moving her arms because of her injured ribs.

Jack went back to the living room and made some call. He called Rene to let him know they made it to Belleville in one piece. Then he called sheriff Dumas to let him know he was back in town. Jack sat down as the sheriff put him abreast of the latest happenings.

It was going to to be difficult to continue with the investigation and take care of Karine, but thankfully, he had Miss Anita. The older woman was a sweetheart, behind the hard exterior was heart of gold. She'd immediately gravitated toward Karine. She'd seen Karin wounded body and immediately went into care taker mode, that was exactly what Karine needed. Jack was pleased that the two of them had hit it off.

He was also pleased to see that Karin's upscale life didn't turn her into a snob. Miss Anita was the help, but Karin didn't care, she just gave the woman the respect that her age deserved. Soledad her mother wouldn't be pleased. With all Karin had been through she'd kept her essence.

Jack new that the wounds in her soul would take years to heal, but for now he was focused on making her better. To that end, Jack told the sheriff about Karine. He was going to need the lawman's help to keep Karine sheltered. This was Roland Dumas town and he needed to know about Raymond and Jack's worry that he might send one of his henchman to Belleville. "I'll keep an eye out Jack, although I'm not sure the fellow will bother he's in enough trouble from what you've told me." "I hope so sheriff, I truly hope so."

Once he'd ended the call Jack went to Karine's room with a glass of water. "Karine it's time for your medication." She took the pills from him, and swallowed them with the water. She laid back down and Jack pulled the covers over her up to her shoulders. She closed her eyes, and drifted back to sleep.

Jack decided to stop by the sheriff's office, since it was only a couple of blocks away from his house. He wasn't planning to stay long because he feared that Karine would wake up disoriented, and she needed to see him there. Miss Anita was kind to her, but she was recuperating from a great trauma and Jack knew that there were bound to be some psychological effects.

The sheriff was on a call when Jack entered the office, Chantale the secretary was at her desk, she smiled at him. "Good morning chief Bourgeois." "Good morning Chantale." "I didn't know you were back in town." "Yeah, I came back just a couple of hours earlier."

"Where the deputy?" "He's out on a call." "The usual, you know a land dispute." Jack shook his head understanding. Until the five women were taken, Belleville's main crimes were land disputes. They were usually settled with the help of the mediator, meaning sheriff Roland Dumas or his deputy Lenny Martin.

"All right Chantale, I'll be in my office for a bit if the sheriff needs me." "Okay chief." She went back to typing the document she was working on. She was an efficient secretary, Jack knew. She was also aware that Chantale was having an affair with the sheriff Deputy.

The man was a married father of three, and although he didn't approve of such behavior, right at this very moment, Jack was painfully aware of the fact that he had a married woman living in his home, and even though nothing was going on between them, Jack couldn't help but wonder if further down the the two of them might get a second chance.

His thought were going along these lines as he was revising the statements made by family and friends of the missing women when his police radio crackled. It was the sheriff's idea, so that Jack could stay informed. Although he'd assisted on a few case, his main focus remained to find out what happened to the women, although he still held out hopes to find them alive, in Jack's experience this was nearly impossible.

It Lenny martin calling in for back up. "I just found the body of a male near the Casimir plantation, I am requesting back up, and I've already called the Doc." Jack dropped the file on his temporary desk, this would have to wait. He exited his office just as sheriff Dumas came out of his.

The two drove to the crime scene separately. Jack followed the sheriff. He was still learning the ins and outs of the small town. Once they got there, Lenny had established a perimeter. Despite the fact that the body was found on the outskirts of town where it was mostly farmland, the nearest house was at a great distance, a small crowd of onlooker had gathered.

"The dead man is Polo Obrien," Lenny told Jack and the sheriff as they approached the body. There was a visible head wound, it looked like blunt force trauma. The dead man was in his late twenties to early thirties Jack surmised. He was obviously murdered since he laid on his front and obvious didn't hit his head by falling.

No, Jack thought, it was no accident. Someone had surprised Polo Obrien and hit him from the back.

Jack breathed a heavy sigh, his case had just gotten complicated because Jack knew the dead man. He'd interviewed him in reference the to disappearance of his fiance Charlotte. The question now was, were the two cases related? Or was there a murderer loose in Belleville?

There were at the crime scene for hours. Jack was forced to remove his jacket, and pull up the sleeve of his blue shirt. It was unusually hot and he was sweating bullet. Since they didn't have a crime scene unit Jack and the sheriff along with the deputy were forced to work the scene themselves.

"Since we didn't have violent crimes out here, the government felt that we didn't need a crime scene unit." "Jack made a mental note to change that. He knew just who to talk to. After all the man owed him, because the simple case was turning out to be anything but.

There wasn't any cell phone service where the scene was, and Jack worried that Karine might wake up feeling disoriented, and he wouldn't be there for her. The medical examiner removed the body after Jack and the sheriff had gathered as much information as they could.

They looked around for the murder weapon, in Jack's opinion was probably a rock. But among the vegetation it was hard. The sheriff concluded that man was probably hit by thick piece of wood, but by the shape of wound Jack deducted it was more like a rock. He did not contradict the sheriff however, he was here on a temporary basis, and he didn't want to step on anyone's toes. The most important thing was to find the killer. As they left the more wooded areas Jack found that he had signal, so he called his home phone. Miss Anita was near by since she answered right away.

"Miss Anita, I am being delayed by work, I wonder if you can stay with Karine until I come back." "In her state I don't want her to be alone." "Say no more Jack, I'll stay with her until you come back." "Okay, then, thank you so much Miss Anita." He made a mental note to pay her the over time. "I'll drive you home when I get back." Jack hanged up the phone before Miss Anita had time to argue.

One of the worst parts of being in law enforcement was showing up at love ones homes and telling them that their son or daughter, husband or wife had been killed. Even after nearly twenty years of police work it was still one of the hardest part of the job as far as Jack was concerned.

Polo Obrien's mother was a small woman in her fifties. The man's father though was as tall as his son had been. As soon as they saw them, Flora Obrien started crying. "They invited Jack and the Sheriff to come in." Their sitting was small and encumbered with too many furniture.

Jack could smell porridge cooking on a wooden stove. They were making supper before settling for the night, and now they were about to shatter the tranquility of their lives forever.

"I knew something had happened to my son," Flora was saying through her tears. It's not like my son to stay out all day." "What happened to my son?, Monsieur Obrien wanted to know. "Was he in accident?" Jack waited for the sheriff to speak. He was new in town, these people didn't know him. In this time of intense distress, it was better for them to learn what happened to their son through someone they knew and were comfortable with.

"No, it wasn't an accident" the sheriff said his face pinched with sadness. "The back of his head was bashed in." Flora broke into a loud sob." "We found him laying on his face, so from that position we can deduct that he was murdered, because if he fell and hist his head we would find him lying on his back."

The father joined in the crying. He held his wife as she sobbed and moaned with pain and grief. "Sheriff, find the person who killed my son, because if I find him first, justice will be done right." It wasn't hard to understand the man's grief and anger, but having him take justice in his own hand would only create more chaos and blood shed.

Vigilanty justice ran rampant along these small towns, and frankly even in the big city. Jack abhorred these type of things, this was why the police force existed, the justice system wasn't perfect, bu

402t Jack believed in it. If he had, he wouldn't have made it his life's work.

As they drove away, Jack could still hear the couple crying. Neighbors had gathered around and Jack knew that at least for the next few days, the family would have the support that they needed.

The sun had set long ago when Jack finally reached home. Miss Anita was waiting for him sitting on the sofa in the living room. She was asleep when he walked in. "Miss Anita, I don't know how to thank you." "It's nothing pitit gasom." "We've had enough on your hand today." It certainly was a long hard day. "I'm going to go check in on Karine then I'll drive you home," Jack told Miss Anita.

Karine was asleep on her side, she had tucked the sheet under her chin and was snoring softly. Jack closed the door behind him quietly, then made his way down the hallway toward the living room. When he reached the living room Miss Anita had her her purse slang over her shoulder.

"Ready to go?" "yes, my taxi is here, she said surprising Jack. "Miss Anita, you called a taxi, I was going to drive you home." "yes, I did, Jack you're falling dead on your feet with fatigue." "Besides, Karine could wake up start worrying." "What you need is a warm shower and a good supper." "Food is on the stove."

"How was Karine today?" "She was fine for the most part." "But she kept screaming her her sleep." "It will be a while before the nightmares go away." She sighed heavily." Jack agreed with the assessment. He hoped that they were keeping Raymond locked up tight, he deserved to be in prison.

The taxi honked, and Miss Anita opened the door. "I'll see you in the morning Jack, get some rest." "I am coming," Miss Anita yelled at the impatient driver who honked his horn again.

Jack checked on Karine once more, before making his way to the bathroom to take a shower. He thought of of the complicated day he had as he washed away the dust and grime.

Belleville was suppose to be the safest town to live, but it was quickly turning into a den of horror. The women were still missing and now there was a dead body. Jack wondered whether they needed to be prepared for the worst case scenario, because this case has sure taken a turn for the worst.

Four

Jack day started early. He postpone his jogging time until Miss Anita was in so he wouldn't leave Karine alone. Yesterday, she'd spent the rest of the day in Miss Anita's company, and Jack wasn't thrilled at the prospect of letting it happen again.

It was an emergency, it often was in this line of work, however he'd brought Karine here to keep her safe, and although the distance was accomplishing it at least partially, Jack still worried.

Raymond might be in jail, but Jack couldn't underestimate how far out he could reach. Dirty money bought a lot of loyalty, and corruption ran rampant in nearly all institutions, including judicial and legal. Jack had no doubt that in his jail cell Raymond was still the king of cocaine.

Rene text him last night that a guard was fired for providing Raymond with a cell phone. Communication with the outside world, that's all Raymond needing to continue running his drug empire. Although the guard had been fired since the man running the prison was a man of integrity, Jack had no doubt that another guard was about to be bought, and the one who'd denounce the dirty guard was now in danger.

For this reason, Jack had Rene approach the man late last night and offer him a job with their company Elite Incorporated. The guard was thrilled at he offer, and was scheduled to meet Rene at their offices around ten o'clock this morning.

Jack checked on Karine again, she was still asleep. She snored softly, the sound reassuring. Jack kept reliving the moment when he'd entered Karine's bedroom, she laid on the floor on her side, her back was to them, so her respiration wasn't noticeable. For a few seconds there, Jack thought that he'd lost her for good, that her bastard husband had murdered her. When he'd turned her over on her back, Jack took her pulse, that was when he'd relieved the breath he didn't even know he was holding. She was still mending, Raymond had hurt her so badly.

Anger simmered on the surface, Jack gritted his teeth. He wanted to punch a wall, but balled his fist instead. Jack knew that eventually he was going to have to do something to ensure that Raymond was never again in close proximity with Karine again.

As soon as Miss Anita showed up, Jack left for his morning jog. He was back in thirty minutes, showered and dressed. He'd called the station to find out what was on the days agenda. It would determine whether Jack drove to work, or walked the few blocks that separated his home from the sheriff's office.

They needed to continue the interviews to solve the Obrien murder, but Jack couldn't loose sight of the fact that the missing women was the main reason why he was in Belleville. So he need to figure out whether the two cases were related. His gut instinct told him that the two cases were related.

However, aside from the fact that the dead man was engaged to one of the missing girls, they didn't have anything else to go on. After a hearty breakfast, Jack left for work. Before leaving the house he went to check on the still sleeping Karine and put aside the medication for Miss Anita to give her.

He drove to work and was surprise to find that the family members of the missing girl were in the sitting room waiting for sheriff Roland Dumas to come in. Jack sent a general **bonjou**r in their direction, and went straight to his office. It was going to be another long day, so he better get started he told himself.

It was just as Jack had predicted, news of the one of the girl's fiance being murdered had arouse new fear. Every one wanted to know what it all meant. Did it mean that for sure their loved ones were deceased. Murdered like the man they found yesterday.

The truth was, no one knew what it meant. Jack couldn't be sure that it meant the girls were dead. But it certainly meant that if the two cases were related that they were now dealing with an abductor capable of murder as well.

www.ingramcontent.com/pod-product-compliance
Lightning Source LLC
Chambersburg PA
CBHW071941120726
48001CB00005B/1995